# A CIRCLE STORY

by Meish Goldish        illustrated by Diane Paterson

## CHAPTERS

**Harcourt**

Orlando   Boston   Dallas   Chicago   San Diego

Visit *The Learning Site!*

**www.harcourtschool.com**

## A Favorite Book

Lisa heard the army base bugler play taps and knew that it was bedtime. She wasn't ready to sleep yet, so she sat up in bed, reading her book. Lisa cherished this book more than any other. The title was *A Horse Called Lucky*.

The story was about a horse that had been a racing champion. He jumped higher and ran faster than the other horses.

Then a farmer bought Lucky and the two plowed the cornfields together. As they got older, they couldn't work as much, so the farmer's son bought a tractor.

After that, the farmer and Lucky spent many days together, walking slowly through the fields, enjoying the outdoors. Then, the farmer had an idea. Just past the farm's fields was a school full of children. On Fridays, he could take Lucky to the school and give the children rides.

While other work horses had shunned the school children, Lucky loved all of the attention. He was happy to let the children ride him if it made them smile.

Lisa knew much of the book by heart, yet she never tired of reading it. While some parts made her laugh, other parts made her cry. The ending was the part she liked most because it always made her feel very happy.

When Lisa first read *A Horse Called Lucky*, many thoughts crossed her mind. She didn't want to forget them, so she wrote notes on small slips of paper. She dated each note and placed it inside the book.

One note read:

> Lucky is a good jumper. I wonder how it would feel to sail over a fence on his back! 7/19/41

Another note read:

> I love Lucky's coat. It reminds me of vanilla-fudge ice cream. 7/20/41

Another note Lisa wrote read:

> Lucky plows such straight furrows in the ground! 7/21/41

The second time Lisa read the book, she added a few more notes. She added some after the third and fourth times, too. No matter how often she read the book, new thoughts always came to her!

This was her latest note:

Finally, Lisa put away her book and went to sleep.

## The Loan

In school, students in Lisa's class were asked to talk about their favorite books. Of course, Lisa gave her report on *A Horse Called Lucky*.

After school, Miguel saw Lisa walking home. He lived a block away from her. Soon, he caught up with her.

"Lisa, I really liked your book report," Miguel said. "Would you mind if I borrowed the book? I'd love to read it."

Lisa smiled. "Sure. I'd be happy to lend it to you," she said.

Miguel went home with Lisa. She took the book from her shelf and gave it to him.

"Thank you," Miguel said. He looked surprised when he saw the slips of paper tucked in the book.

"Lisa, what are these?" he asked.

Lisa laughed. "Those are notes I write each time I read the book. They help me to remember what I like about it."

Miguel smiled. "You sure like to write notes!" he joked.

"Yes, I do," Lisa agreed. "Because I don't want to write in the book, I put my thoughts on paper slips instead."

"What a great idea!" Miguel said. "Thanks for lending Lucky to me."

Miguel took the book and went home. Lisa felt good that someone else was now reading *A Horse Called Lucky*, and she hoped that Miguel would enjoy the story as much as she did.

On Monday, Lisa wanted to ask Miguel how he liked the book. She looked for him, but he wasn't in class. "Maybe he's sick," Lisa thought.

Miguel was out of school for the rest of the week. Finally, Lisa called him at home. The operator told her that the number was no longer in service. Lisa thought she might have dialed the wrong number, but when she called again, the same thing happened.

Lisa was puzzled. She walked to Miguel's block and was surprised to see that his house was empty. There was even a "Vacant" sign in the front yard.

Lisa tried to find out where Miguel's family had gone. She asked neighbors on the block. Then the next day, she asked her teacher.

"Miguel's father was transferred to another army base," said Miss Jones. Because Miguel had to move quickly, he had been unable to return her book. Lisa feared that the book she cherished was gone forever.

## SURPRISE MAIL

Lisa never heard from Miguel. Over time, she almost forgot about *A Horse Called Lucky*. There were so many other books to read.

Lisa grew up and went to college. Soon, she got married. She and her husband had two children. Lisa read many books to her children. She tried to find a copy of *A Horse Called Lucky*, but no bookstore or library had it.

One day she placed an ad in the newspaper asking if anyone owned a copy of *A Horse Called Lucky*. Unfortunately, she got no response.

Many years later, a package addressed to Mrs. Lisa Parker arrived in the mail. Lisa was curious about the package because she wasn't expecting to receive anything in the mail. She carefully removed the paper to see what was inside.

Lisa gasped. She couldn't believe what she saw! It was her old copy of *A Horse Called Lucky*. A letter was attached to it.

July 7, 2001

Dear Mrs. Parker,

Our family has had this book for many years. My brother, sister, and I read it. So did my parents, aunt, uncle, and cousins. Mama gave us the book. She got it from Grandpa Miguel. I feel lucky to have read this book.

Grandpa told me the book really belonged to you. I am returning it. Sorry it is so late. I drew a family tree to show you who read it.

Sincerely,
Maria Gonzales

The book was stuffed with notes! It was twice as thick as before. Lisa couldn't believe its growth! One note read:

> Sometimes I feel lonely, just like Lucky.
>
> Juan 10/13/71

Another note read:

> The ending makes me so happy!
>
> Maria 2/19/01

Many people had read and enjoyed her favorite book over the years. It had gone from person to person to person. Finally, like a circle, the book had come back to Lisa to stay.